A Marc Brown ARTHUR Chapter Book

Muffy's Secret Admirer

Text by Stephen Krensky
Based on a teleplay by Sandra Willard

Little, Brown and Company
Boston   New York   London

Copyright © 1999 by Marc Brown

First Edition

The characters and events portrayed in this book are fictitious. Any
similarity to real persons, living or dead, is coincidental and not intended
by the author.

Arthur® is a registered trademark of Marc Brown.

Text has been reviewed and assigned a reading level by Laurel S. Ernst,
M.A., Teachers College, Columbia University, New York, New York;
reading specialist, Chappaqua, New York

Library of Congress Cataloging-in-Publication Data

Krensky, Stephen.
    Muffy's secret admirer / text by Stephen Krensky ; based on a
teleplay by Sandra Willard. — 1st ed.
        p.   cm. — (A Marc Brown Arthur chapter book ; 17)
    Summary: Brain and Francine devise the perfect plan to get even
with Muffy after she bribes the judges at the science fair.
    ISBN 0-316-12017-0 (hardcover). — ISBN 0-316-12230-0 (pbk.)
    [1. Revenge Fiction.   2. Practical jokes Fiction.   3. Aardvark
Fiction.   4. Animals Fiction.]   I. Title.   II. Series: Brown, Marc Tolon.
Marc Brown Arthur chapter book ; 17.
PZ7.K883Mu   1999
[Fic] — dc21   99-35312
                                                                      CIP

10 9 8 7 6 5 4 3 2 1

WOR (hc)
COM-MO (pb)

Printed in the United States of America

For Michael Barron

Chapter 1

· · · · · · · · · ·

"It's not fair!" said Francine.

She was sitting with Arthur, Binky, and the Brain on the stairs outside the school auditorium. They had just finished showing their exhibits at the science fair.

Arthur wiped some white dust off his face. "Mine probably would have made a better impression if it hadn't exploded," he said.

Francine laughed. "You mean you didn't do that on purpose?"

Arthur shook his head. "I told D.W. not to fool around with the ingredients." He

1

cupped his chin in his hands. "But I don't think she listened to me."

The Brain nodded knowingly. "Well, my experiment didn't explode, but it might as well have. There's no chance I can win now. And I really wanted that award for the best exhibit."

"So did I," Francine admitted.

"You can still do it," said Arthur. "Any of you."

"No way," said the Brain. "Muffy's going to win for sure. You saw what happened. When she served pastries to the judges, they made all those happy noises."

"And they were big pastries," said Binky, licking his lips. "Covered in whipped cream and filled with all kinds of good stuff."

"But that shouldn't matter," said the Brain. "Even if they were from the best bakery in town and served on fine china with linen napkins."

"Which, of course, they were," Francine noted.

The Brain folded his arms. "They had nothing to do with her project. Nothing at all."

"That wouldn't bother Muffy," Arthur reminded them. "You know how her mind works. She thinks money can buy anything."

"Well," Francine admitted, "it does seem to buy most things. But this should be different!"

The Brain agreed. "It's a crime, a mockery of our educational system. I mean, I worked for weeks on my Blackboard of the Future . . ."

"And I worked for days on my Lessons from Lunch nutrition poster," said Francine.

"Don't forget me," said Binky. "I worked for minutes, at least two or three, collecting rocks near school for my Rocks near School diorama."

The Brain frowned. "If there is true justice in the world, Muffy won't get away with this. Judges should not be swayed by gooey fillings."

"Maybe they won't be," Arthur said hopefully.

"Ha!" said the Brain.

"But what can we do?" Francine sighed. "The laws of science don't seem to apply to Muffy."

Binky pounded his right hand into his left. "There are other forms of persuasion," he reminded them.

"Trying to outdo Muffy won't improve the situation," said Arthur. "She can outspend all of us put together."

"Arthur is right," said the Brain.

"I am?" asked Arthur.

"Absolutely." The Brain folded his

arms. "We can't compete with Muffy on her own terms. We have to find another approach."

"Like what?" asked Francine.

The Brain frowned again. He seemed to be doing that a lot. "I don't know yet," he said. "It's going to require further thought. But I know one thing . . ."

He stood up abruptly and thrust his fist toward the sky.

"I'm going to get . . . *revenge!*"

Chapter 2

• • • • • • • • • • • •

Wanting revenge was one thing, but figuring out the right kind of revenge was something else. At recess, the Brain sat on the playground trying to determine his next move.

Francine sat next to him.

"Maybe I could make Muffy's teeth turn green," he said. "Some kind of spinach potion, perhaps."

Francine considered it. "Green would clash with most of Muffy's outfits," she said. "And Muffy would hate that. But remember, she has that new solar-sonic toothbrush. She could probably just brush the green away."

"I'd forgotten about that toothbrush," the Brain admitted. "Wait . . . wait! Imagine this: Muffy is riding along on her bike, picking out property she plans to buy someday. Suddenly, a big magnet appears over her head. She tries to pedal faster, but she cannot escape. The magnet gets closer and closer. Then it grabs hold of the bicycle and lifts it and Muffy into the air." He smiled. "I can hear her screams already."

"That would give her a good scare," Francine agreed. "But where are you going to get a big magnet? And what will hold it up? A helicopter? And where are you going to get that?"

The Brain looked pained. "Give me a little time. I didn't say I had worked out *all* the details."

Francine snorted. "You're going to need more than a little time," she said.

Arthur came over to join them. "I can see by your faces that your revenge plan isn't making much progress."

The Brain just growled at him.

Arthur shook his head. "Brain, you have to let go of this. If you don't, you'll go crazy and your brilliant scientific career will be ruined before it even starts."

"Go away," said the Brain. "I can't talk to you. I must concentrate all my thinking capacity on the task at hand."

"They haven't even announced the winner yet," Francine reminded him. "Who knows? Muffy might lose."

The Brain snorted.

"Sometimes it's better to forgive and forget," said Francine. "Be noble. Turn the other cheek. Stuff like that."

"Stuff like what?" asked Muffy, who was passing by with Prunella.

"Oh, nothing," said Francine.

"By the way," said Muffy, "I still have a

few pastries left over. Does anybody want one?"

Francine and the Brain said nothing.

"Maybe later," said Arthur.

"They're really good," Prunella told them.

Muffy smiled. "You should know—you had three. Francine, *you* might like ... oh, right, I forgot. With your new interest in nutritional values, pastries are probably a bad idea." Muffy shuddered. "Honestly, Francine, I don't know where you got that idea. Who wants to know all that food-group stuff? I eat what I like and I like what I eat."

Prunella laughed. "That's a good one, Muffy," she said.

"Food for thought," Muffy added.

Prunella laughed again. Then they walked off together.

Francine glared after them both. "I may

10

have been too hasty," she said, turning to the Brain. "Maybe we shouldn't give up on revenge just yet."

Chapter 3

• • • • • • • • • • •

The kids returned to Mr. Ratburn's class after recess. Muffy was still talking with Prunella.

"So I'm trying to decide where to put the award. There's a nice spot in my bedroom, but not as many people will see it there."

"Maybe the living room would be better," Prunella suggested.

"You may be right. Over the grand piano would be worth considering. I'll ask—"

She stopped suddenly, seeing a folded piece of paper on her desk. "What's this?"

she wondered aloud. She opened it and started to read.

"What is it?" asked Prunella.

Muffy didn't answer. She just kept reading and reading and reading. Then she gathered Prunella, Sue Ellen, Francine, and Fern.

"You won't believe what I got," she said.

"A new bike."

"An entertainment center."

"A trip around the world."

"No, no," said Muffy. "I mean here at school. It's a note."

"What kind of note?" asked Sue Ellen.

Muffy smiled. "You be the judge," she said. "Listen to this. 'Dear Muffy, I have long admired you. Regardless of the difference in our ages —' That means he's older."

"How can you tell?" asked Sue Ellen.

"If he was younger," said Fern, "he wouldn't know how to write."

Prunella wasn't so sure. "Maybe he's a genius kindergartner," she pointed out.

"Puh-leeze," Muffy said. "There's more. 'I had to make my feelings known. You are so mature, so stylish. I think about you every day. Your smile, your laugh, the way your clothes stay so crisp and the colors never fade. I hope you return my feelings. Sincerely, Your Secret Admirer.'"

Muffy sighed. She pictured herself having a picnic with her dream guy in the back of one of their matching Rolls Royces or going down to the bank to count each other's money.

"Maybe he's even in *fifth* grade."

Prunella shook her head. "Any fifth-grader who would write a letter like that is nuts."

"I don't think so," Muffy insisted. "He obviously appreciates maturity and fine clothes."

Prunella shrugged.

Muffy grabbed Francine's arm. "Let's watch the fifth-graders and figure out who wrote the note."

"I can't," said Francine. "I have cafeteria duty."

"All right, then, you come with me, Sue Ellen."

Sue Ellen groaned.

Francine smiled to herself as they walked away.

The Brain watched all this from another table. A smile slowly spread across his face.

"What are you so happy about?" Arthur asked him. "You look like one of those cats that swallows the canaries. All that's missing is the feathers."

The Brain tapped his fingers together. "Have you ever realized how easy it is to manipulate someone into doing what you want?"

Arthur shook his head. "That never works with D.W. Believe me, I've tried."

The Brain said nothing.

"Brain, you're acting kind of weird today."

"Am I?" He laughed. It was like a laugh of a mad scientist from some old horror movie.

And it gave Arthur a chill.

Chapter 4

• • • • • • • • • • •

Francine was stacking trays in the cafeteria. All around her, people were talking.

"Did you hear about Muffy's note?" asked Fern. "I think the paper was very expensive."

"And I heard the writer used gold ink," said Sue Ellen.

"Real gold?"

"Well, if you wanted to impress Muffy, that would be the right way."

"Very true."

Francine was amazed. Gold ink? How had they come up with that?

"Francine?"

Arthur was standing beside her.

"Did you hear the Brain cackling on the other side of the room?" he asked.

"Cackling?" Francine tried to look surprised. "I may have heard him laugh from time to time. He seems very happy about something."

"And are you happy, too?" Arthur asked. "I haven't heard you cackle."

Francine stacked up a few more trays. "Just because the Brain's happy doesn't mean I am."

"It does if you have the same reason to be."

Francine blinked innocently. "Arthur, what are you talking about?"

"I'm talking about you and the Brain. Working as a team. Together."

"The Brain? Me? Us? Working together? On what?"

"Getting back at Muffy," said Arthur. "The two of you wrote that note to her."

"Note? What note?"

"The note from Muffy's secret admirer."

Francine looked around nervously. "What makes you think I was involved?"

Arthur folded his arms. "Well, it could be that I have great powers of deduction."

"Or?"

"Or it could be that I can read minds and yours is coming in loud and clear."

"Or?"

"Or it could be that I saw you put the note on her desk."

Francine's protest died in her throat. "Oh. I guess that would be kind of a clue. But what about the Brain? He wasn't with me."

Arthur snickered. "Only he could use 'regardless' correctly in a sentence. Besides, you two have been huddled together all morning. So, why did you do it?"

"Because Muffy was acting so superior

about the science fair. And you have to admit, Arthur, that her exhibit was no better than anyone else's. But she wasn't willing to take her chances like everyone else. No, she had to influence the judges. And the worst part is, that doesn't even bother her. Whatever Muffy wants, Muffy gets." Francine paused. "Well, now she is getting something else she wants."

"But this isn't a real thing," Arthur reminded her. "It's something you and the Brain invented to make her look silly."

Francine didn't try to argue. "And it's working, isn't it? Look at her — running around with that dopey expression on her face. Muffy, the girl who has everything, now has something even she didn't expect."

"But what if she finds out you did it?"

Francine bit her lip. "Are you going to tell her?"

Arthur considered that for a moment. "I

don't want to get caught in the middle of this. But I have a bad feeling about it, Francine. I think you should tell her yourself before it's too late."

Francine stuck her nose in the air. "Fat chance," she said.

Chapter 5

• • • • • • • • • • •

"What's the matter, Muffy?" Francine asked as Muffy stormed over to her during afternoon recess.

"What's the matter? I'll tell you what's the matter. Sue Ellen is trying to steal my secret admirer."

"Really? I didn't know you had already figured out who it is."

"Well, not completely," Muffy admitted. She pointed to a game of kickball. "But I've narrowed it down to someone playing in that game. Sue Ellen and I were discussing the possibilities when the ball was kicked to us. She kicked it back and they asked her to play. Now she's showing off."

"So?" said Francine.

"So my secret admirer is out there. What if he's impressed by her brute strength?"

"I'm sure he's more loyal than that," said Francine.

"Well, I don't want to take any chances. This secret-admirer business can be very tricky, Francine. I can't wait too long to answer him."

Francine fidgeted a little. "But he's a *secret* admirer, Muffy. Maybe he wants to keep it that way."

Muffy dismissed this idea with a wave of her hand. "Oh, I don't believe that. It was just a way to get my attention."

"So what will you do?"

Muffy had that figured out. "I'm going to hire Buster right away. He's a detective.

He can find out who it is. Then I won't have to wonder anymore."

Francine looked worried. Buster was a pretty good detective. He had once figured out the truth about Arthur and the missing quarters. What would he discover this time? Had she left any clues for Buster to find?

Francine and the Brain were standing in the prisoners' box before the judge. They each wore striped pajamas and had a ball and chain attached to an ankle.

The judge sat on a high bench before them. He was wearing a powdered white wig, but there was something familiar about him.

"You look like my teacher Mr. Ratburn," Francine told him.

"Silence!" roared the judge. "In my court, you will speak only when ordered to do so. Continue, sir."

He pointed to Arthur, who was interviewing a witness. Arthur was wearing a wig, too. He kept wrinkling his nose. Francine decided the wig powder must be itchy.

"Your name, please," said Arthur.

"Buster Baxter."

"And your occupation?"

Buster sat up straight in the witness chair. "Private detective," he said. He handed Arthur a business card and gave one to the judge, too. "No case is too small," he boasted, "to occupy my full attention."

"Yes, yes," said Arthur. "Now tell us, Mr. Baxter, what did you discover after being hired by Muffy Crosswire?"

Buster consulted a small notepad. "After getting this assignment, I quickly determined that Francine and the Brain were responsible." He looked up at Francine. "It was child's play."

The judge slammed down his gavel.

"That's all the evidence I needed to hear. Guilty as charged!"

As Francine and the Brain were dragged from the courtroom, Francine called out, "It was just a joke!"

But nobody even smiled.

Chapter 6

Francine found the Brain sitting against a tree. He was drawing in his notebook. Francine could just make out a stick figure inside a laboratory during a thunderstorm before the Brain closed the cover.

"Don't you love it when a plan comes together?" he said.

"Our plan isn't coming together," she told him. "It's falling apart."

"Impossible!" The Brain stood up. "We cannot fail!"

Francine snorted. "You hope. Maybe our letter was a little too convincing. I mean, it really stirred up Muffy's curiosity.

She can't wait to find out who her secret admirer is."

"Of course not. That's what we had hoped."

"I know. But we didn't hope that she would hire Buster to investigate."

The Brain paused for a moment. "Unexpected, but not important. Buster's good, but he'll never trace anything to us. A detective needs clues to learn something. And I'm too clever to have left any clues."

"Oh, really? Well, Arthur figured out that you wrote the note. He didn't think anyone but you could use 'regardless' correctly."

The Brain was not impressed. "Just a fluke," he maintained. "Now for Phase Two." He consulted his notebook. "We need to take the next step. Which do you prefer, candy or flowers?"

Francine glared at him. "What's wrong

with you? We're in a big enough mess already. I don't want it to get any bigger."

The Brain just laughed.

The mad scientist, Dr. Brain, straightened his lab coat as he stood at the computer-screen blackboard finishing an equation.

"Dealing with Muffy Crosswire will be the final test before I unleash my plan for taking over the world." He cackled wildly as lightning flashed outside the window. "Isn't that right, my loyal assistant?"

From the shadows, a peasant girl in rags stepped out. "I guess so, master," Francine said quietly.

"Louder!" shouted Dr. Brain.

"I can't," she said.

"And why not?"

"Because I'm not sure."

Dr. Brain turned on her. "Not sure? Not sure? You dare to question me?"

Francine cringed at his tone, but she

wouldn't change her mind. "This Crosswire girl worries me," she went on. "She is used to getting her way."

"So am I!" Dr. Brain reminded her.

"Oh, yeah . . . that's why we're stuck doing experiments in this crummy dungeon." Francine looked down. "And, boy, do I need a bath."

"Silence!" cried Dr. Bruin.

"Earth to Brain, Earth to Brain!" Francine snapped.

The Brain rubbed his eyes. "Sorry," he said.

"As I was saying," Francine continued, "I think maybe we made a mistake."

"Just remember," said the Brain, "*we* didn't start this, Muffy did."

"Well, what are we going to do about it?"

"Tell the truth," said Arthur, coming up

behind them. "It's your best chance to keep the situation from getting worse."

"We're not that desperate," the Brain insisted.

Francine wasn't so sure. "Not yet," she muttered.

Chapter 7

· · · · · · · · · · ·

On the other side of the playground, Buster stood quietly, thinking.

"Hey, Buster!" cried Muffy.

Buster didn't answer. He was staring at the ground.

"Helllllo!"

Buster finally looked up. "I'm concentrating," he explained.

"That's good," said Muffy. "Now stop and tell me what you've found out about my secret admirer."

Buster cleared his throat. "It's too bad you waited so long to hire me."

"I didn't wait! This all happened today."

Buster shook his head. "Time is not the same for detectives as it is for other people. Anyway, I've examined the note. It's handwritten."

"I knew that."

"In block letters to disguise the handwriting."

Muffy rolled her eyes. "I knew that, too."

"Then I examined your desk, which we detectives refer to as the crime scene."

"And . . ."

Buster shrugged. "Unfortunately, the area has been contaminated. Too many fingerprints, footprints . . ."

"Hmmmph!" said Muffy. "Are you saying you've discovered *nothing?*"

"Did I mention the block letters?"

Muffy groaned. "Some detective you are. If I had paid you already, I'd be asking for a refund."

* * *

As Muffy and Buster talked, Francine and the Brain watched from behind the tire swings.

"Look at them," said Francine. "Going over every detail. Figuring out each part of our scheme."

"It really wasn't that complicated," said the Brain.

Francine bit her lip. "Let's confess before it's too late! We can throw ourselves on the mercy of the court."

The Brain's eyes narrowed. "You're being unrealistic. They'll never take us alive."

Francine threw up her hands. "Well, now I feel *much* better. What a mess this stupid note has caused. I wish we'd never written it."

"Hey, Francine!" Arthur came running up to them. "Has Buster interviewed you yet? He's working his way through the class."

Francine blinked. "I know I'll crack like an egg under his questions." She looked down. "There I'll be, in little pieces all over the playground."

The Brain sighed. "The thrill of revenge seems to be short-lived," he admitted. "I suppose we should clear this up and apologize."

Francine brightened. "You mean it?"

"I'll try," said the Brain. "How about this?" He cleared his throat. "Muffy, I'm sorry I allowed myself to get upset about the way you bribed the judges."

Arthur frowned. "I don't think that's quite right," he said. "It's missing a certain something . . ."

"Like crawling on our knees and begging for forgiveness," said Francine.

The Brain cleared his throat again. "Yes, yes, I see your point. Let me try again . . . Muffy, I'm sorry I couldn't let a huge injustice go unpunished. But I guess I had no choice."

Francine just shook her head. Clearly, they had a long way to go.

Chapter 8

● ● ● ● ● ● ● ● ● ●

By the end of lunch, Francine was just about worn out. She had tried to make progress with the Brain, but her efforts had not been rewarded.

"I thought I was doing better," said the Brain.

Francine shook her head. "Calling Muffy a fast-talking bamboozler is not doing better."

"Did I hear my name?" asked Muffy, coming around the corner.

"No!" Francine and the Brain said together.

"Oh, well . . . it doesn't matter." She

beamed at them. "I have important news! I found out who wrote the note."

"You did?" said Francine. "Well, we can ex—"

"And I've taken steps to follow up," Muffy went on.

"Steps?" the Brain repeated. "What kind of steps?"

"I wrote a note back saying that while he has good taste, a love between us can never be."

"That's quite a note," Francine admitted. "Can I see it?"

"Oh, no," said Muffy. "I already put it in his locker."

Francine and the Brain gasped.

"An impulsive decision," said the Brain.

"Very," added Francine. "Whose locker did you put it in?"

"Rattles's."

"Rattles's?" said the Brain. "The kid with all those muscles, even in his head?"

Muffy nodded. "Poor thing. I know I'm breaking his heart. But when you fall in love, you take your chances. Well, see you later."

She walked off, leaving Francine and the Brain gasping for air.

"This really *is* a mess," the Brain admitted.

"I'll say," said Francine. "Rattles will pulverize her if he reads that note."

"I tried to warn you," said the Brain. "Writing that note was ill advised."

Francine gaped at him. "You tried to warn *me*?"

The Brain smiled weakly.

"Never mind," he said. "This is no time for finger-pointing. It's time for action."

He led Francine to Rattles's locker.

"Now what?" asked Francine. "We're on the outside and the note is on the inside."

The Brain pressed his eye to the vents. "I can't see anything."

Francine scratched her head. "What if we stick some gum to a piece of string and then drop the string through the vent? The note might stick to it and we could pull it out."

"You actually think that would work?"

Francine shrugged. "It's our last hope."

"When you put it like that," said the Brain, "I say we give it a try. Where's your gum?"

Francine quickly chewed a stick of gum and attached it to some string from her pocket.

"Here goes . . ."

She tried to push the gum through one of the slots. Unfortunately, it got stuck on the way.

"Uh-oh," she said.

"Wait a minute," said the Brain. He opened his backpack and took out a piece of wire. "I have this left over from my science experiment." He fished the wire

under the locker door. "If we're lucky, the note is sitting on the bottom. I may be able to snag—ah! I've got something."

He brought out a piece of paper.

"That doesn't look like —" Francine began.

"It's not," said the Brain. "This is a page from a bodybuilding magazine." He sighed. "But Rattles won't be building any bodies in the near future. He'll be taking some apart."

"And why is that?"

Francine and the Brain jumped around. Rattles was standing before them.

Chapter 9

• • • • • • • • • • •

"I'm not going to ask you again," Rattles said. "What are you doing at my locker?"

"It's a good question," said Francine.

"Excellent," the Brain agreed. "Concise. To the point. Even—"

"I'm waiting . . ." said Rattles.

"Would you believe we're here because of the nice view?" the Brain asked.

"No."

"How about that we're big fans?" said Francine. "And we were waiting around to get your autograph?"

"I don't think so," said Rattles. "Why

would you be fans of mine all of a sudden? I haven't done anything special lately."

Francine looked at the Brain. "Your turn," she said.

"I'm thinking," he replied.

Suddenly, Muffy appeared behind Rattles.

"What's going on here?" she asked.

"I found these two trying to break in to my locker," Rattles explained.

"Really?" said Muffy.

"And I keep asking them why, but I haven't gotten the right answer yet." He folded his arms. "And time is running out."

"Well, before it does," Muffy said calmly, "I should tell you that they're here because of me."

Rattles stared at her. "Oh, yeah? So then maybe I should hold you responsible."

He took a threatening step toward her.

"Now, now," said the Brain, darting be-

tween them. "Let's not be hasty. It's all my fault."

"And mine," said Francine. "So if you must pulverize someone, make it me."

"You see," the Brain explained, "we were mad at Muffy and wrote her a fake love note. She thought you wrote it and wrote you a note back. Now it's in your locker— but you probably shouldn't read it."

He and Francine looked at Rattles for a reaction.

"You expect me to believe a ridiculous story like that?"

"It's not ridiculous," Francine insisted.

"Use your imagination," the Brain suggested. "That's what we did."

Suddenly, Rattles started laughing. Then Muffy laughed, too.

Francine wanted to laugh with them, but first she wanted to know what was so funny.

"Did we miss something?"

"You should have seen the looks on your faces," said Rattles.

"It's priceless," said Muffy. "Well, maybe not priceless, but certainly worth a lot."

Rattles agreed. "You were right, Muffy! They really did think you put a note in my locker! Oh, brother!"

"I think we've been set up," said the Brain.

Francine looked at Muffy. "You mean you knew we wrote the note?"

"Not at first. That's why I hired Buster. But I also noticed how worried Arthur looked every time he talked to you. And he kept mumbling about 'telling the truth.' So I added things up. Then I asked Rattles for a favor."

Francine wanted to say something. She was partly mad and partly relieved.

The Brain, however, had a thought. "Revenge," he said sadly, "is very over-rated."

Chapter 10

• • • • • • • • • • •

As the bell rang, everyone filed back into class.

"We're sorry we wrote the note," said Francine, having finally gotten over her shock.

Muffy nodded. "Well, I can understand why you did it."

"You can?" said the Brain.

"Certainly. You were upset that I'm better than you at science."

The Brain took a deep breath. "You may be better at winning contests, but you're not better at science."

Muffy stopped to think about this.

"I don't see the difference," she said.

"All right, everyone," said Mr. Ratburn, "take your seats. It's time to announce the winner for the best display in the science fair."

He held up a sheet of paper.

"The judges voted for the display that was . . . well, let's say one of the tastiest—"

Muffy raised her hand. "Excuse me, Mr. Ratburn?"

"Yes, Muffy?"

"I just wanted to say that I've been thinking."

"There's something new," the Brain muttered.

Francine elbowed him in the side.

"The Brain's project really was more scientific than mine," Muffy went on. "I think he deserves the award more than I do."

"Oooooh!" the class cried out.

Mr. Ratburn cleared his throat. "Well, Muffy," he said, "I suppose that's very noble of you."

"I guess she's not so bad, after all," the Brain whispered to Francine. "I feel like a dope."

"Unfortunately," Mr. Ratburn continued, "you didn't win the contest, so I'm afraid the award isn't yours to pass along."

"What?" cried everyone.

Muffy turned as red as a ruby ring.

"As I was saying," Mr. Ratburn went on, "the winner of the award for the best entry in the science fair is . . . Francine Frensky."

He handed Francine a handsome plaque, which she displayed on her desk.

The Brain turned to her in surprise.

"You? All this time I was worried about Muffy, and *you* turned out to be the competition? How is that possible?"

Francine smiled sweetly at him. "Maybe you just need to learn to cook," she said.

The Brain just rolled his eyes.

"Congratulations, Francine," Muffy said quietly. "The way things turned out, maybe I would have been better off with a secret admirer, after all."

Francine smiled at her award. "Well, as you said before, it's food for thought."